Will and the *Magic* Snowman
Adventures in St. Paul

Written by
Gloria Fjare Dunshee
Illustrated by
Karne Dunshee McGary

WillGo PRESS
www.WillGoPress.com

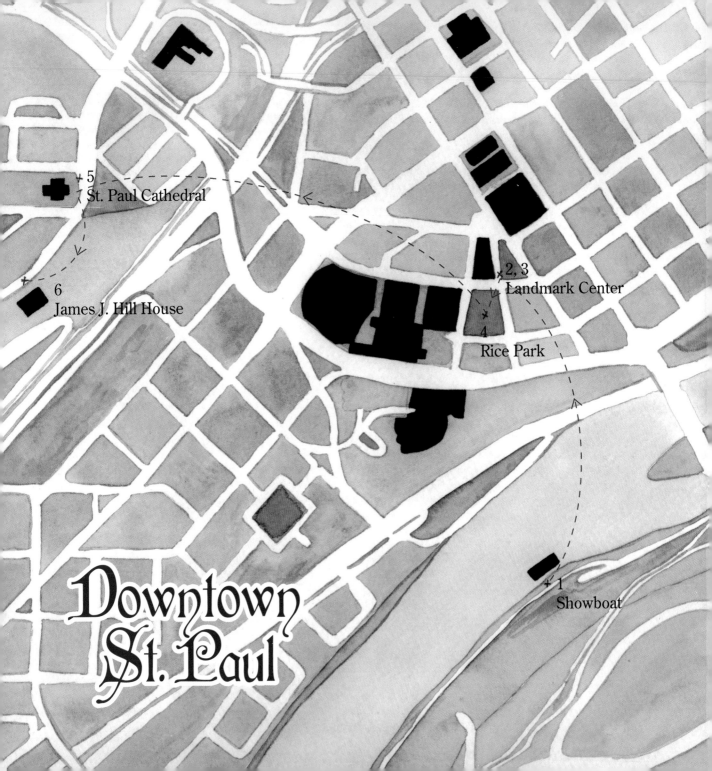

+ 5
St. Paul Cathedral

+ 6
James J. Hill House

2, 3
Landmark Center

4
Rice Park

+ 1
Showboat

Downtown
St. Paul

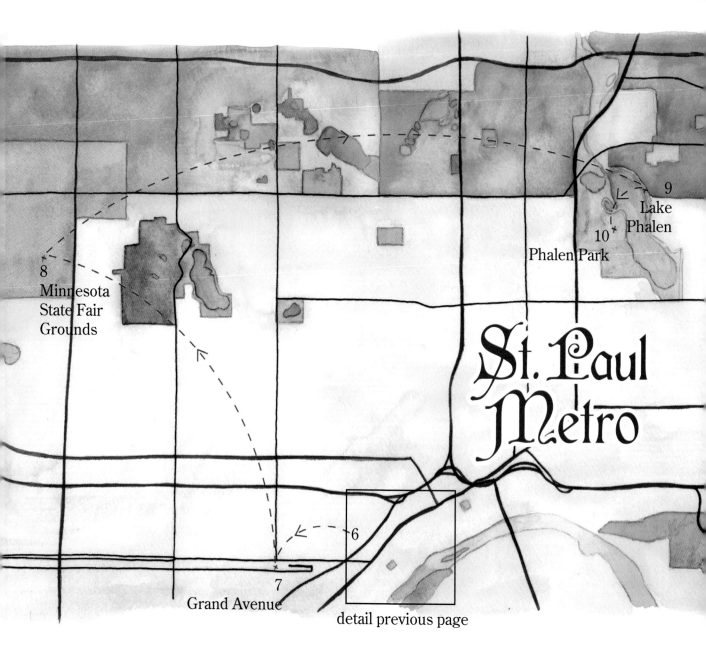

8
Minnesota
State Fair
Grounds

9
Lake
Phalen

10
Phalen Park

St. Paul
Metro

6

7

Grand Avenue

detail previous page

It was nearly Thanksgiving Day. William was sad.
As he looked out the window, how could he be glad?
He looked up in the sky. He looked down on the ground.
As he looked all around, not a flake could be found.
The leaves were all gone. The trees were all bare.
The ground should be white, but the snow wasn't there.

Mommy was baking and planning and cooking.

William was wishing and hoping and looking.

He remembered the snow that fell from the sky,

How it covered the buildings and trees way up high.

He would wear mittens, a scarf, and a hat,

His boots, a warm coat, and all of that.

2

It seemed like a dream now, the moon when it snowed.
It was just like magic to see how it glowed.
His memories of winter were vivid and clear.
He wished that the snow was already here.

As he gazed out the window, his head on his arm,
He started to dream. He was cozy and warm.
He was startled to find himself standing outside.
The trees were all snowy, piles of snow by his side.
It was cold. He was shivering, and he stared all wide-eyed.
As he looked all around, he smiled and he sighed.

Now this is more like it, he thought as he smiled.

There was snow everywhere. It was drifted and piled.

He was down by the river. He saw a big boat.

He started to wonder, now where was his coat?

Mommy said that he needed to wear it outside.

But wait, what was that by the river he spied?

5

Smiling and holding his
coat was a snowman.
And this was where
William's adventure began.
A little black nose, a hat on his head,
Arms that were sticks,
and eyes that were red.
William walked over, looked up, and said, "Please,
Mr. Snowman. I must have my coat, or I'll freeze."
"My name is Anders," he said as he grinned.
"Here is your jacket, my cold little friend."

6

Will took his jacket and put it on fast.

His cold little arms would be warmer at last.

It was snowy and cold, and the sun was so bright.

The steam on the air was fluffy and white.

He took Anders' hand and away they did go.

They flew towards the tall buildings covered in snow.

They arrived at a place
where people were skating.
There were mommies
and daddies and
children all waiting
To put on their skates
and sail round the rink.
It looked like such fun
and he started to think.
He thought going
out on the ice
would be grand.
But Anders was
holding so tight
to his hand.

When he turned around
he felt very small.
For there was a nutcracker
standing so tall.
Anders walked over and
reached for the hat.
He lifted it off and
gave William a pat.
"Now this should feel better"
he said as he turned.
"Your head is so cold;
and I was concerned."
So Will took the hat and
pulled it down snug.
It felt warm on his head.
He gave Anders a hug.

9

They walked past the skaters and on down the street.
There were new things to see, and people to meet.
As they came down the block, William had to look twice.
There were all kinds of statues made out of ice.
The first one he saw was a dog and a boy.
The boy was handing the doggie a toy.

When he walked further along he saw fish in a school.
They were sitting at desks and not in a pool.
It made William smile, giant fish made of ice.
He was having such fun. He thought, this is nice.

Way up ahead, now what did he see?
A smiling ice cat, on a great big ice tree.
A big caterpillar was sitting upright.
Both cat and caterpillar were shiny and bright.
Will wanted to touch them. They looked so inviting.
Nestled into the trees and holiday lighting.

Anders asked Will if he
wanted to go,
There was so much more
that he wanted to show.
Up ahead he could see a
large church on a hill.
As they walked
closer he was
getting a chill.

He saw a stable with shepherds and wise men,
Mary, and Joseph, and sheep, at least ten.
The baby looked cold. He walked closer to see.
Up there, by the manger, what could it be?
There were his boots sitting right in plain sight.
He pulled them on quickly as he sat in the light.
Behind them were buildings, one with a dome.
All were covered in white snow that looked just like foam.
He breathed in the crisp air and looked at the sight.
The sky was so blue. The snow was so white.

There were many great mansions with snow all around.
There were many great sights to amaze and astound.
He wondered who lived in these wonderful places,
With porches and gates and great fireplaces.
He imagined princes and kings and governors too.
He saw houses with gates, brown, white and blue.
All of the houses were covered in snow.
Some were decked out in lights that did glow.
Anders just smiled as he held William's hand.
William had never seen things quite so grand.

As they continued they came to some shops.
There was snow everywhere, even on the treetops.
Shoppers in overcoats were carrying big bags.
There were babies in strollers, and presents with tags.

Everyone was hurrying around and around.
But Will was enthralled with the sights and the sounds.
The next thing he knew, they were flying away,
To a field where snow artists were busy at play.

19

They were standing on top of a hill, in the wind.
As he looked all around at the sculptures, he grinned.
He felt like an ant standing next to the statues.
They were all made of snow and were meant to amuse.
There were three massive snowmen, holding a sign.

20   Towering over Anders they looked oh, so fine.

And then he looked up and he saw a friend.

With an ear and an arm gone, he needed a mend.

As William got closer he had a surprise.

There were some mittens that were just his size.

They were lying on top of a snow statue's arm.

He pulled them on fast. They were fuzzy and warm. 21

But they took off very fast, before he could blink.
They were down by a lake, right next to a rink.

And then he remembered the light show last year.
They drove through the park. There were lights far and near.
Santa was driving a truck filled with toys.
The peacock was wondrous with lights all turquoise.

They walked slowly under a string of bright lights.
They had seen very many wonderful sights.
What fun, how exciting the things he had seen.
He tried to remember just where he had been.

When William awoke he let out a cry.
There was snow on the window,
coming down from the sky.
A squirrel on the railing
was looking inside.
He seemed to be looking
for somewhere to hide.
Will bounced to his feet
and ran closer to see.
The snow was piled
high, almost
deeper than he.

Will was so glad for the snow that was here.
Then he looked out in the yard for the deer.
God sent the snow that made everything white.
He cared for the animals, both day and night.
And then Will was startled. What did he hear?
It was Gracie, his cousin.
She was walking quite near.

Tonight they would have
so much fun, wait and see.
Tomorrow, they'd go sledding out by the tree.
They would build a big snowman, like Anders, his friend.
They could make snow angels. The fun would not end.
But now Will was thankful for other good things.
He had family who loved him and all that it brings.
There was snow in the winter, bright leaves in the fall.
He was grateful to God for sending it all.
Tonight he was thankful for family and food.
He would watch all the snow. It was all very good.

1. The Minnesota Centennial Showboat, owned and operated by the University of Minnesota, is used for summer theater productions.

6. The James J. Hill House was built by railroad magnate James J. Hill. It is listed as a U.S. National Historic Landmark.

2. The Landmark Center originally held many government offices after its completion in 1902, but now houses an arts and culture center for St. Paul.

7. Grand Avenue is a charming St. Paul shopping area (stretching 30 blocks) with lots of one-of-a-kind shops and local restaurants.

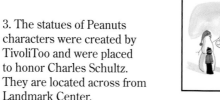

3. The statues of Peanuts characters were created by TivoliToo and were placed to honor Charles Schultz. They are located across from Landmark Center.

8. A snow sculpture contest on the Minnesota State Fair grounds has also been part of past Winter Carnivals.

4. An ice sculpture contest in Rice Park has been part of past Winter Carnivals, held each year in January and February.

9. Ice fishing takes place on many, if not most, Minnesota lakes during the winter from the time the ice is thick enough to hold you.

5. The St. Paul Cathedral is on a hill overlooking downtown St. Paul. Each Christmas season, a nativity scene is placed in front of the cathedral.

10. A holiday lights display has been put up for several years in Phalen Park, adjacent to Lake Phalen in Maplewood.